MUSIC
CLASS
TODAY!

Music Class Today!

Music and lyrics by DAVID WEINSTONE

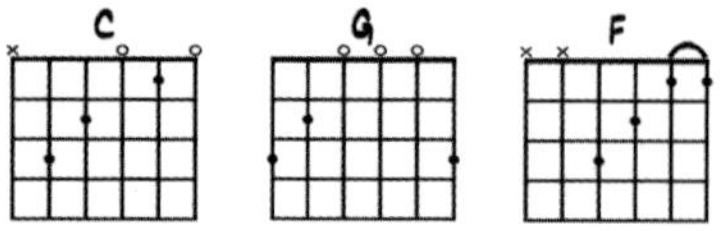

INTRO:

C   G   C
HELLO, JOHN. HELLO, SUE. HELLO, BILLY. HELLO, YOU!
C   F   G   C
HELLO, MAYA. HELLO, RUE. HELL-O, EVERYBODY! IT'S GOOD TO SEE YOU.

VERSE 1:

C   G   C
SHAKE YOUR EGGS HIGH! SHAKE YOUR EGGS LOW! ONE ROLLED AWAY—WHERE DID IT GO?
C   F   G
TIME FOR A SONG. EVERYONE SING! I THINK I'LL JUST WATCH . . . BUT I'M LISTENING!

CHORUS:

C   F   G   C
THAT'S ALL RIGHT, THAT'S OKAY. WHEN-EVER YOU'RE READY, COME ON OVER AND PLAY.
C   F   G   C
THAT'S ALL RIGHT, THERE'S NO RUSH. WHEN-EVER YOU'RE READY, COME PLAY WITH US!

VERSE 2:
CHORUS:
VERSE 3:
CHORUS:
VERSE 4:

(SPOKEN):

C   F   G   C
GOOD FOR YOU, THAT'S THE WAY. EVERYBODY'S IN THE BAND! HOO-RAY!

TAG 1:

F   C   G   C
CLEANUP TIME. PLEASE LEND A HAND. THANKS SO MUCH. THIS DAY'S BEEN GRAND.

VERSE 5:

TAG 2:

C   F   C   F   G
BUT I LOVE MUSIC CLASS! I DON'T WANT TO SAY GOODBYE. MY FROGGY WANTS TO STAY—AND SO DO I!

OUTRO:

C   F   G
THAT'S ALL RIGHT. THAT'S OKAY. WE'LL SEE YOU SOON ANOTHER DAY!
C   F   G   C
THAT'S ALL RIGHT. THAT'S OKAY. WE'LL SEE YOU SOON ANOTHER DAY!

VERSE 2:

KICK YOUR FEET HIGH! KICK ONE, THEN TWO.
SNEAKERS FLY! WHO LOST A SHOE?
TIME FOR STICKS. GO CLICKETY-CLACK.
I THINK I'LL JUST WATCH . . . HERE ON YOUR LAP.

VERSE 3:

TWIRL YOUR SCARVES, SPIN AROUND AND AROUND.
DID SOMEONE GET DIZZY AND HAVE TO SIT DOWN?
A COUNTING SONG—COUNT ONE, TWO, THREE!
I THINK WE'LL JUST WATCH—MY FROGGY AND ME.

VERSE 4:
(SPOKEN)

EVERYBODY'S DANCING AND HAVING A BALL.
WHO IS THE SILLIEST DANCER OF ALL?
PLAY-ALONG TIME—COME JOIN THE FUN!
WELL, I THINK I WILL. WAIT HERE TILL I'M DONE!

VERSE 5:

SO GOODBYE, JOHN. GOODBYE, SUE.
GOODBYE, BILLY. GOODBYE, YOU!
GOODBYE, MAYA. GOODBYE, RUE.
GOODBYE, EVERYBODY—IT WAS GOOD TO SEE YOU!

Music Class Today!

A Music for Aardvarks Book

David Weinstone

Pictures by Vin Vogel

FARRAR STRAUS GIROUX
New York

For Ezra, Roman, and Milo
—D.W.

To Nook, Sherman, Teddy, and Peppermint Patty,
who share the office with me and have
to tolerate my loud music
—V.V.

Farrar Straus Giroux Books for Young Readers
175 Fifth Avenue, New York 10010

Text copyright © 2015 by David Weinstone
Pictures copyright © 2015 by Vin Vogel
All rights reserved
Color separations by Embassy Graphics
Printed in China by Toppan Leefung Printing Ltd.,
Dongguan City, Guangdong Province
Designed by Roberta Pressel
First edition, 2015
1   3   5   7   9   10   8   6   4   2

mackids.com

Library of Congress Cataloging-in-Publication Data
Weinstone, David.
    Music class today! / David Weinstone ; pictures by Vin Vogel. — First edition.
        pages cm
    "A Music for Aardvarks production."
    Summary: A group of toddlers enjoys a lively music class, including, at last, one very
shy two-year-old boy.
    ISBN 978-0-374-35131-1 (hardback)
    [1. Stories in rhyme.   2. Music—Instruction and study—Fiction.   3. Musical
instruments—Fiction.   4. Bashfulness—Fiction.]   I. Vogel, Vinicius, 1972–   illustrator.
II. Title.

PZ8.3.W42433Mus 2015
[E]—dc23
                                                                                          2014040693

Farrar Straus Giroux Books for Young Readers may be purchased for business
or promotional use. For information on bulk purchases please contact Macmillan
Corporate and Premium Sales Department at (800) 221-7945 x5442
or by email at specialmarkets@macmillan.com.

One rolled away—

Where did it go?

Time for a song.

Everyone sing!

That's all right, that's okay.
Whenever you're ready,
come on over and play.

That's all right, there's no rush.
Whenever you're ready,
come play with us!

Kick your feet high!

Kick one, then two.

That's all right, that's okay.
Whenever you're ready,
come on over and play.

That's all right, there's no rush.
Whenever you're ready,
come play with us!

Twirl your scarves,

spin around and around.

Did someone get dizzy

and have to sit down?

zzz...

A counting song—Count
one, two, three!

That's all right, that's okay.
Whenever you're ready,
come on over and play.

That's all right, there's no rush.
Whenever you're ready,
come play with us!

Everybody's dancing and having a ball.

Who is the silliest dancer of all?

Play-along time—
come join the fun!

Good for you, that's the way.

Everybody's in the band!

Hooray!

Cleanup time.
Please lend a hand.

Thanks so much.
This day's been grand.

Goodbye, Maya.
Goodbye, Rue.

Goodbye, everybody—
it was good to see you!

That's all right, that's okay.
We'll see you soon another day!